The Three Billy Goats Gruff

Retold by M. J. York

Illustrated by Molly Idle

The Child's World®
1980 Lookout Drive · Mankato, MN 56003-1705
800-599-READ · www.childsworld.com

Acknowledgments
The Child's World®: Mary Berendes, Publishing Director
The Design Lab: Kathleen Petelinsek, Design
Red Line Editorial: Editorial direction

ISBN 9781614732150
LCCN 2012932806

Printed in the United States of America
Mankato, MN
July 2012
PA02125

Once upon a time, three billy goats lived together in a meadow on a mountaintop. The three billy goats were brothers, and their last name was Gruff.

All spring and all summer, the three billy goats ate grass together. They ate so much grass that they ate all the grass in their meadow. The three billy goats were hungry. They needed to find a new meadow.

There was a meadow on a nearby mountain. This meadow was thick with sweet, green grass. A rushing river lay between the three billy goats and the meadow. The three billy goats would have to cross an old, creaky bridge to reach the green grass.

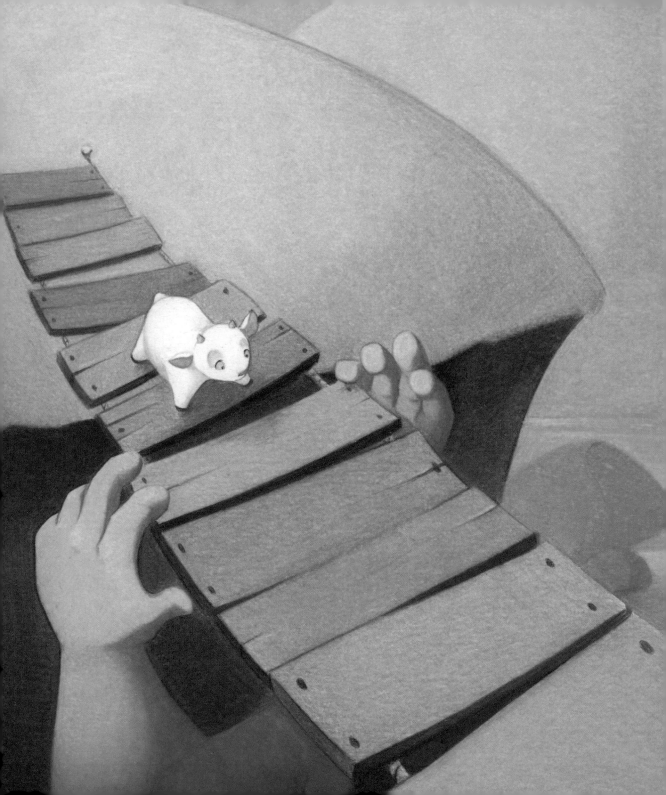

Little Billy Goat Gruff agreed to cross first. He took one step on the bridge. He took two steps, and then three steps. His steps went "trip-trap, trip-trap" on the creaky bridge. He shook the bridge just a little bit as he crossed.

Suddenly, a voice roared out, "WHO'S THAT TRIP-TRAPPING OVER MY BRIDGE?" Two big, ugly hands reached up from under the bridge.

Little Billy Goat Gruff
trembled. "It is I, Little Billy
Goat Gruff," he said in his
smallest voice.

A big, ugly troll jumped up
on the bridge. "I'M GOING TO
EAT YOU!" roared the troll.

"No, don't eat me!" squeaked Little Billy Goat Gruff. "I'm too little to eat. My brother is coming soon, and he's much bigger than I."

The troll paused and scratched his head. He looked at Little Billy Goat Gruff. "You're too small for a snack," he said. "You may cross the bridge." And Little Billy Goat Gruff ran to the meadow as fast as he could.

A little while later, it was Middle Billy Goat Gruff's turn to cross the bridge. He took one step on the bridge. He took two steps, and then three steps. His steps went "TRIP-TRAP, TRIP-TRAP" on the creaky bridge. He shook the bridge a lot as he crossed.

Suddenly, a voice roared out, "WHO'S THAT TRIP-TRAPPING OVER MY BRIDGE?" Two big, ugly hands reached up from under the bridge.

Middle Billy Goat Gruff
stopped in his tracks. "It is I,
Middle Billy Goat Gruff,"
he said.

The big, ugly troll jumped
up on the bridge. "I'M GOING TO
EAT YOU!" roared the troll.

"No, don't eat me!" said Middle Billy Goat Gruff. "I'm too little to eat. My brother is coming soon, and he's much bigger than I."

The troll paused and scratched his head. He looked at Middle Billy Goat Gruff. "You're too small for lunch," he said. "You may cross the bridge." And Middle Billy Goat Gruff ran to the meadow as fast as he could.

Finally, it was Big Billy Goat Gruff's turn to cross the bridge. He took one step on the bridge. He took two steps, and then three steps. His steps went "TRIP-TRAP, TRIP-TRAP" on the creaky bridge. His steps shook the bridge so much that he almost shook it down.

Suddenly, a voice roared out, "WHO'S THAT TRIP-TRAPPING OVER MY BRIDGE?" Two big, ugly hands reached up from under the bridge.

Big Billy Goat Gruff kept walking. "It is I, Big Billy Goat Gruff," he said.

The big, ugly troll jumped up on the bridge. "I'M GOING TO EAT YOU!" roared the troll.

"No, you're not!" said Big Billy Goat Gruff. He lowered his head and ran at the troll. He caught the troll on his horns and threw the troll right off the side of the bridge. The troll tumbled into the water and was never seen again.

Big Billy Goat Gruff
crossed the bridge and found
his brothers in the meadow.
And the three billy goats ate
the sweet, green grass together
for the rest of the year.

ABOUT THE AUTHOR

M. J. York has an undergraduate degree in English and history, and a master's degree in library science. M. J. lives in a brick house like the Three Little Pigs and bakes bread like the Little Red Hen.

ABOUT THE ILLUSTRATOR

Molly Idle lives in Arizona with her brilliant husband, two mischievous boys, and two snuggly cats. When not making mischief with her boys, Molly can be found in her studio making books.